DEDICATIONS

Mom and Dad, thanks for instilling in me, Jeff, and Rai the importance of making a difference.

All of my family, thanks for your continuous love and support.

Jolena, it was a blessing to be able to work with a phenomenal writing coach and editor.

In memory of Dad, Jeff, and Wan, the world is a better place because of the difference you made in the lives of others.
C.E.D.

Copyright Information
©
Corey Elizabeth Dean
All Rights Reserved

"What counts in life is not the mere fact that we have lived. It is what difference we made in the lives of others..."

Nelson Mandela

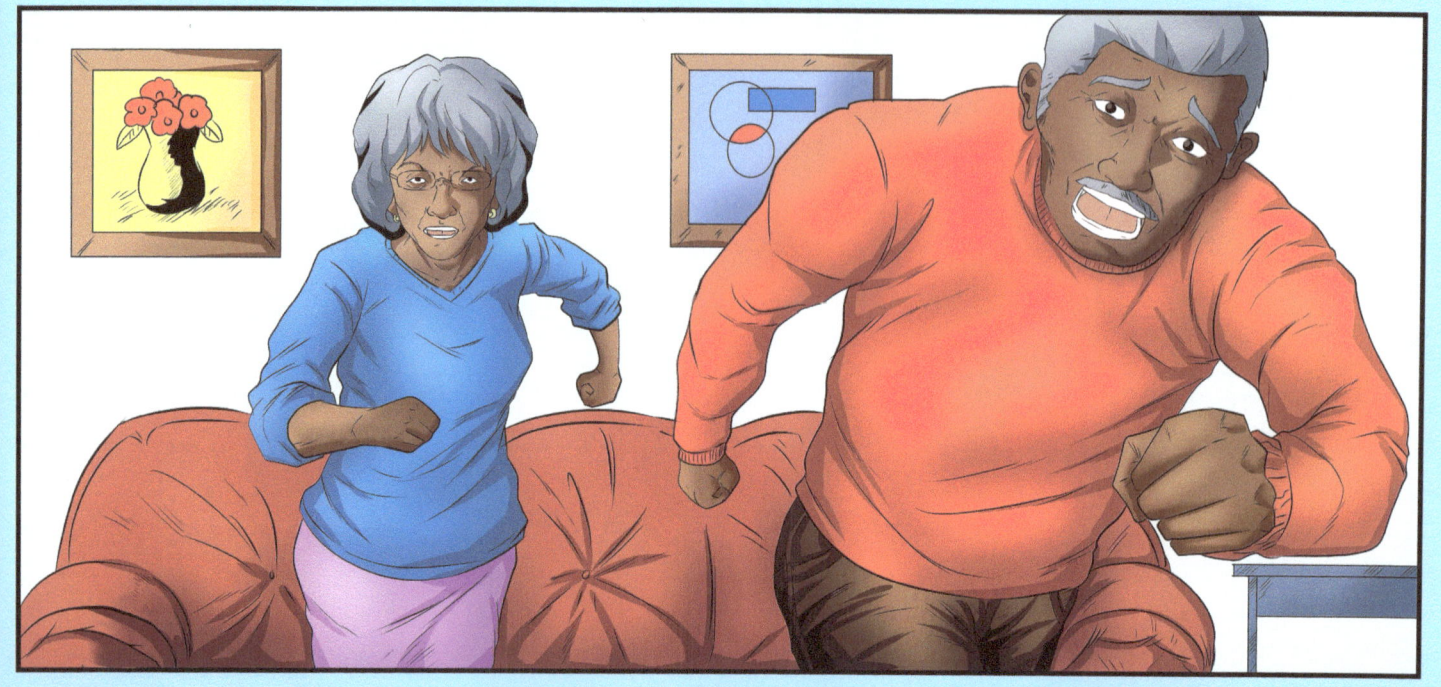

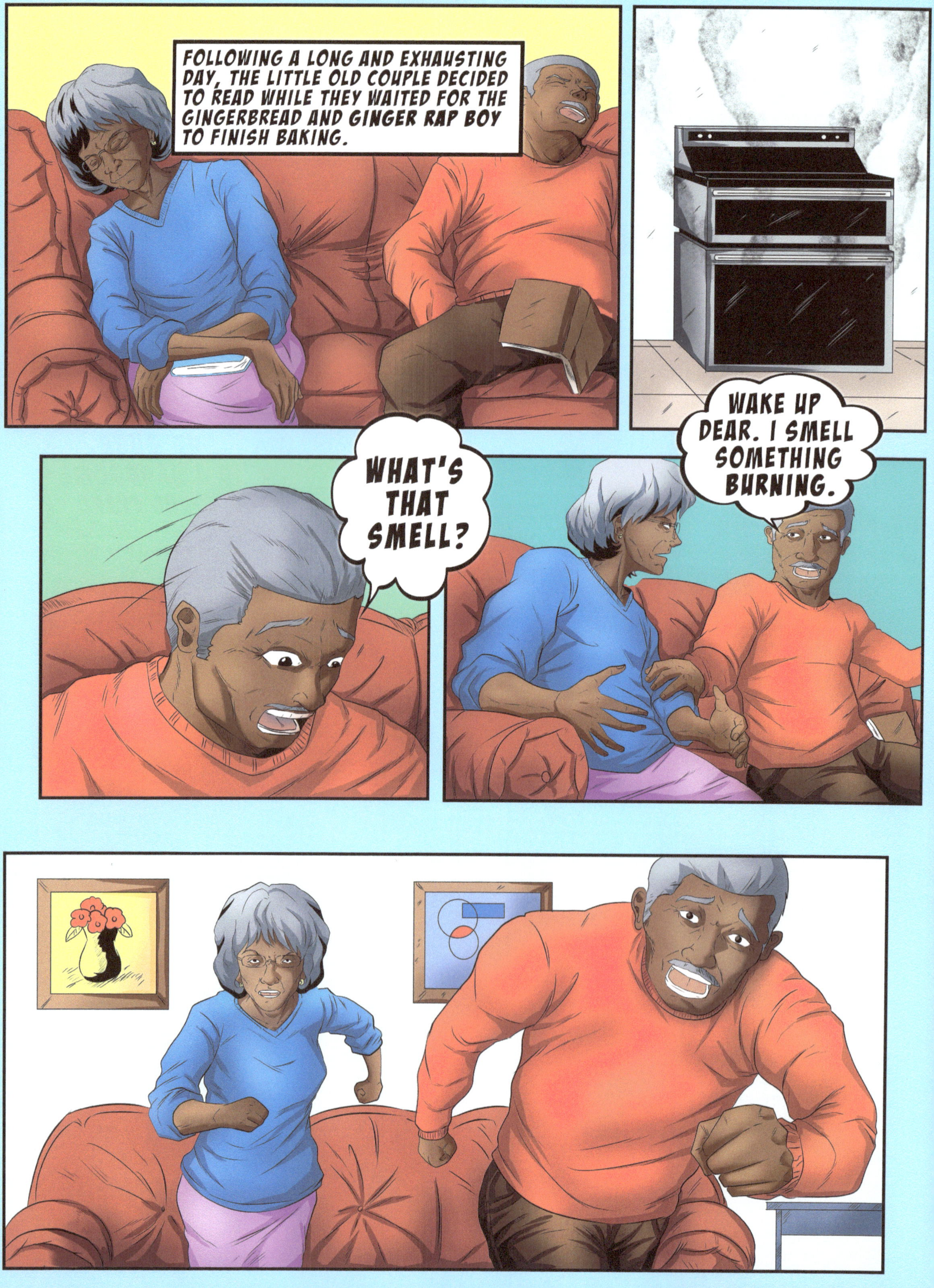

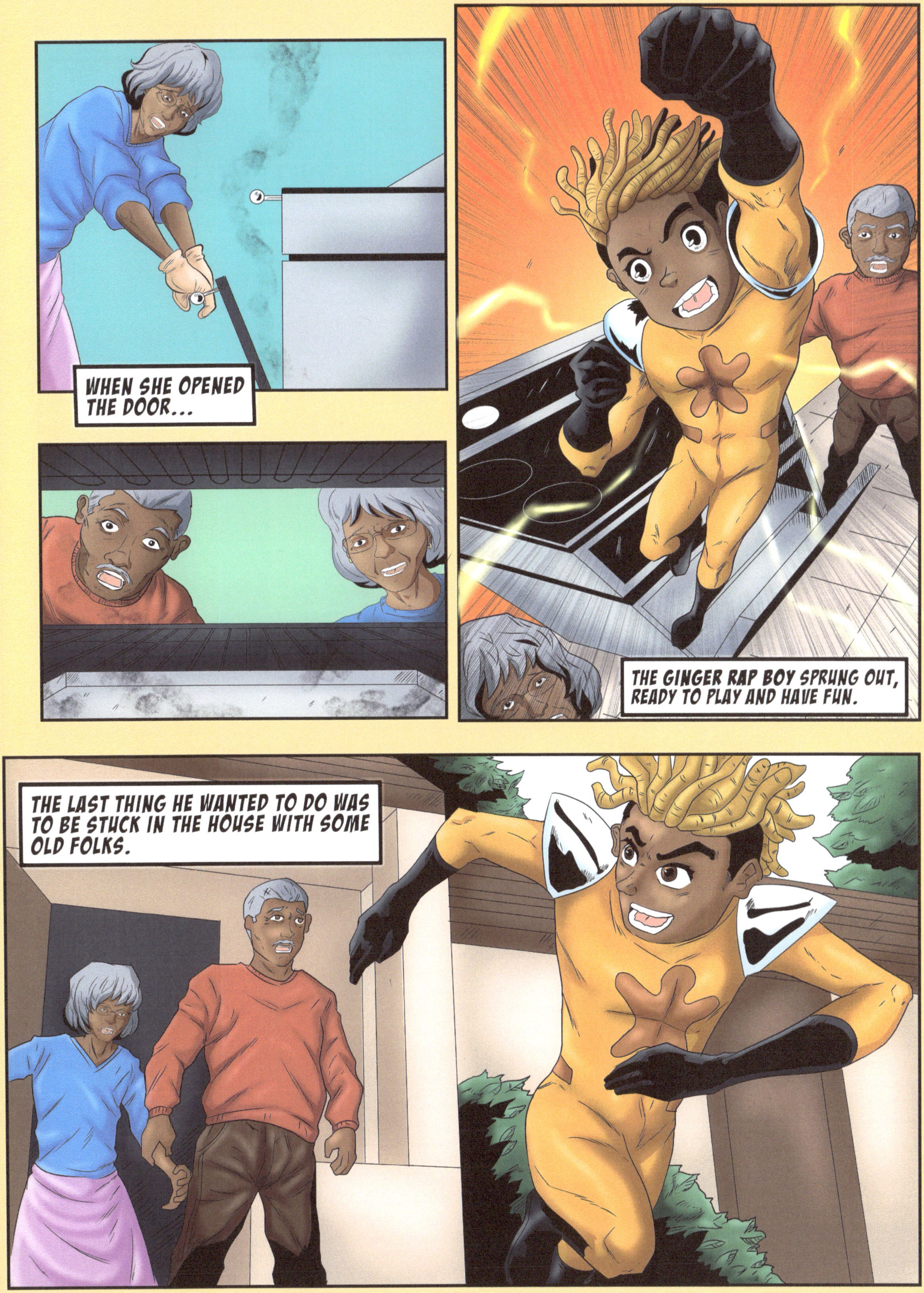

WHEN SHE OPENED THE DOOR...

THE GINGER RAP BOY SPRUNG OUT, READY TO PLAY AND HAVE FUN.

THE LAST THING HE WANTED TO DO WAS TO BE STUCK IN THE HOUSE WITH SOME OLD FOLKS.

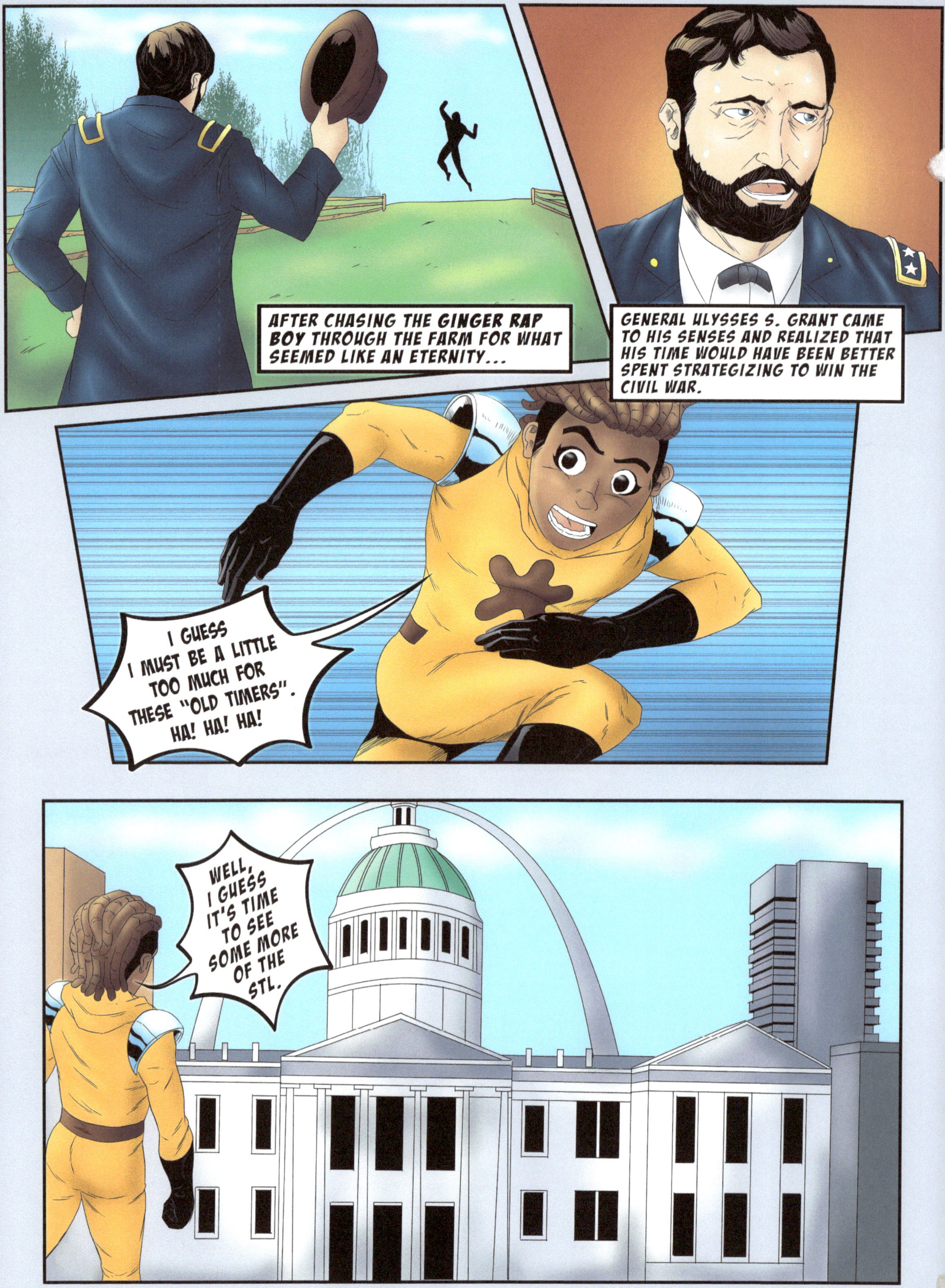

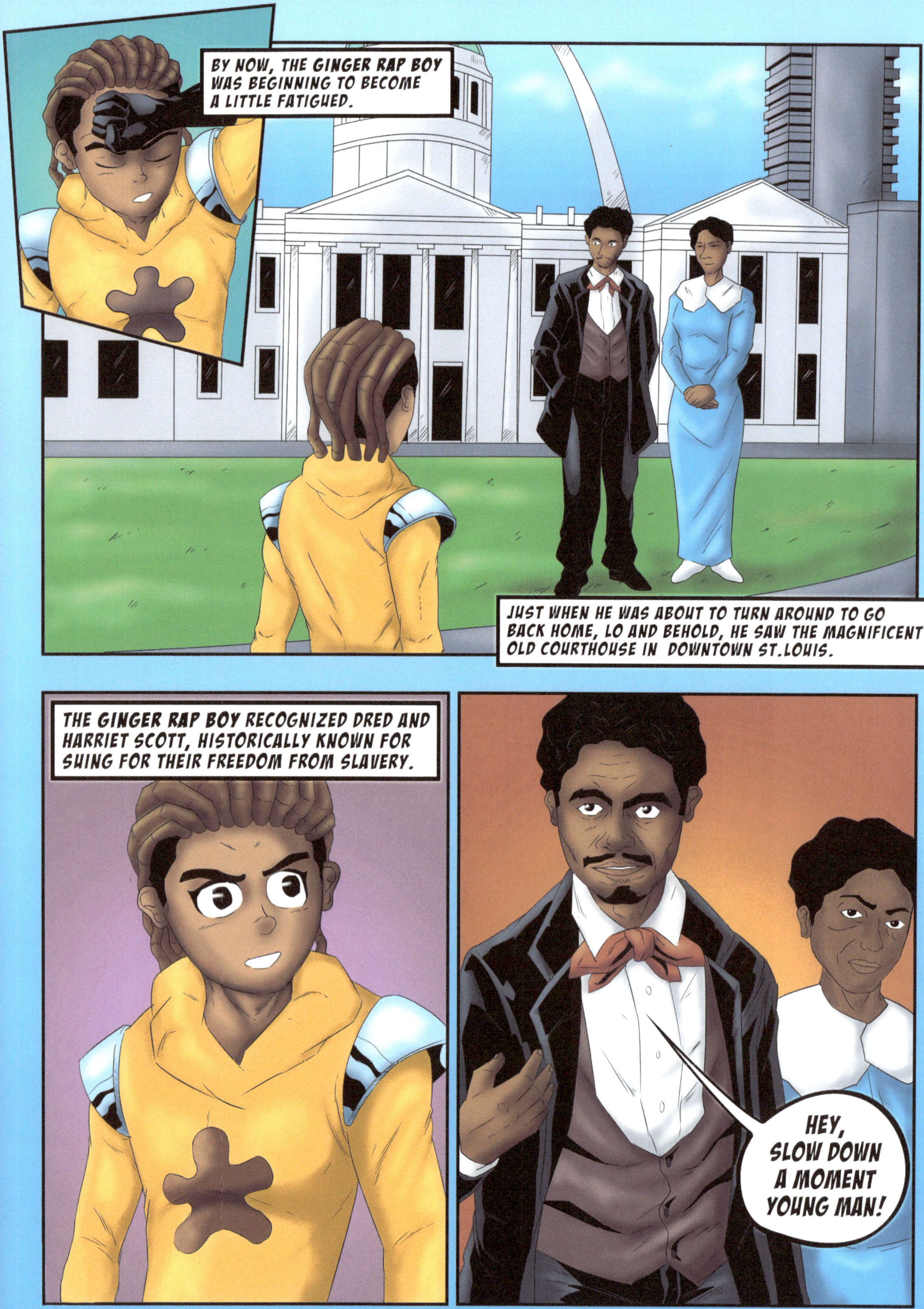

Panel 1: MY WIFE AND I NOTICED THAT YOU SEEMED TO HAVE LOST YOUR WAY AND WE WOULD LIKE TO HELP YOU OUT.

Panel 2: HMMM. NOT INTERESTED.

Panel 3: I'VE ALREADY RUN AWAY FROM A LITTLE OLD WOMAN, A LITTLE OLD MAN, GENERAL ULYSSES S. GRANT AND SCOTT JOPLIN. I WILL RUN AWAY FROM YOU TOO.

Panel 4: RUN, RUN, RUN FOR JOY. YOU CAN'T CATCH ME - I'M THE GINGER RAP BOY!

THINK ABOUT IT

/ WHO IS GENERAL ULYSSES S. GRANT? HOW DID HE MAKE A DIFFERENCE? WHAT ST. LOUIS FAMILY ATTRACTION IS NAMED AFTER HIM?

/ WHO IS SCOTT JOPLIN? HOW DID HE MAKE A DIFFERENCE?

/ WHO ARE DRED AND HARRIET SCOTT? HOW DID THEY MAKE A DIFFERENCE?

/ WHO IS BARACK OBAMA? HOW DID HE MAKE A DIFFERENCE?

/ HOW CAN THE GINGER RAP BOY MAKE A DIFFERENCE IN HIS CITY, COUNTRY, AND THE WORLD?

/ HOW CAN YOU MAKE A DIFFERENCE IN YOUR CITY, COUNTRY, AND THE WORLD?

GLOSSARY

ABANDON (ə-ban-dən)
TO LEAVE BEHIND WITH NO PLAN TO RETURN OR TAKE POSSESSION AGAIN

BARBEQUE (bar-bə-kyu)
SPELLING OFTEN USED IN THE MIDWEST FOR BARBECUE OR BBQ

CHAP (CHap)
A BOY OR MAN

ENCOUNTER (en-koun-ter)
TO MEET SOMEONE OR SOMETHING UNEXPECTEDLY

FATIGUED (fə-tēgd)
DRAINED OF STRENGTH AND ENERGY

FRACTURED FAIRY TALE (frak-CHərd fer-ē tāl)
A REWRITTEN FAIRY TALE THAT CHANGES THE SETTING, CHARACTERS, EVENTS, AND LANGUAGE

HISTORICALLY (hi-stȯr-i-k(ə-)lē)
CONCERNING WHAT HAPPENED IN THE PAST

MAGNIFICENT (mag-ni-fə-sənt)
SOMETHING OF EXCEPTIONAL SIZE OR BEAUTY

PONDERING (pän-d(ə-)ring)
THINKING ABOUT SOMETHING DEEPLY AND CAREFULLY

PURSUIT (pər-süt)
THE ACTION OF FOLLOWING OR PURSUING SOMEONE OR SOMETHING

SCENIC (sē-nik)
HAVING PLEASING OR BEAUTIFUL SCENERY

STRATEGIZING (stra-tə-jīz-ing)
TO MAKE UP A STRATEGY OR PLAN

SCURRY (skər-ē)
TO MOVE QUICKLY, ESPECIALLY WITH SMALL RUNNING STEPS

STROLL (strōl)
TO WALK IN A SLOW, RELAXED MANNER

WAFT (wäft)
TO CARRY OR CAUSE TO GO GENTLY ON WATER OR THROUGH THE AIR

ABOUT THE AUTHOR

COREY ELIZABETH DEAN IS A DISTINGUISHED EDUCATOR WHO HAS A BACHELOR OF SCIENCE IN EDUCATION DEGREE AND A MASTER OF ARTS IN TEACHING DEGREE. SHE HAS SERVED AS BOTH A CLASSROOM TEACHER AND A LIBRARIAN AND IS THE RECIPIENT OF SEVERAL AWARDS FOR EXCELLENCE IN TEACHING. AFTER RETIRING FROM PUBLIC SCHOOL EDUCATION, SHE HAS CONTINUED TO UTILIZE HER TEACHING EXPERTISE BY WORKING WITH DISADVANTAGED STUDENTS AND TEACHING IN THE PRISON SYSTEM. THIS IS HER FIRST CHILDREN'S BOOK.

ABOUT THE ILLUSTRATOR

FITRIA NURKARIMA IS A PROFESSIONAL FREELANCE CARTOONIST, ILLUSTRATOR, AND CONCEPT ARTIST. HE HAS A BACHELOR OF ARTS IN ILLUSTRATION AND A BROAD RANGE OF EXPERIENCE IN TRADING CARD GAMES, COMIC BOOK COLORING, LINE WORK, GAME ASSETS, PIN-UPS, POSTERS, BOOK COVERS, CHARACTER DESIGN AND CONCEPT DESIGN.

MAKE A DIFFERENCE

Milton Keynes UK
Ingram Content Group UK Ltd.
UKHW050718231124
451587UK00002B/36